Bunya the Witch

by

ROBERT KRAUS · MISCHA RICHTER

Little Simon
Published by Simon and Schuster Inc., New York

For Bruce and Billy
and Sacha

Little Simon

Simon & Schuster Building
Rockefeller Center
1230 Avenue of the Americas
New York, New York 10020

Text copyright © 1971 by Robert Kraus
Illustrations copyright © 1971 by Mischa Richter
Published by the Simon & Schuster Juvenile Division
LITTLE SIMON and colophon are trademarks
of Simon & Schuster Inc.
Manufactured in the United States of America

10 9 8 7 6 5 4 3 2

Library of Congress Cataloging in Publication Data

Kraus, Robert, 1925–
  Bunya the witch.
  (Windmill paperbacks)
  SUMMARY: Strange things occur when the old lady
living on the edge of town discovers her magical powers.
  [1. Witches—Fiction] I. Richter, Mischa, 1910–
II. Title.
PZ7.K868Bu 1980   [E]   80-13252

ISBN 0-671-68422-1

Once upon a time, there was a very tiny old lady and her
name was Bunya. Tiny Bunya lived alone in a very old tumble-
down cottage on the outskirts of a small village.
Every day all the children of the village came to
Bunya's to tease and torment her.
"Bunya, Bunya,
You're a witch!
Bunya, Bunya,
Dig a ditch!"
chanted all the children.
"Sticks and stones
will break my bones
but names will never hurt me." Bunya chanted back.

So the children threw sticks and stones
as well as mud at her.
"Witch! Witch!" they cried as they threw.

"I'm not a witch!" cried Bunya. "I'm *not!* I'm *not!*"
"Okay, Bunya," said a loud boy. "If you're not a witch,
prove it!"
"That's right," said his friend. "If you're not a witch,
prove it!"
"Prove it! Prove it! Prove it!" screamed all the children.

"Prove that I'm not a witch?" said Bunya. "Who can prove
they're not a witch?"
"If I *was* a witch, *that* I could prove. I would make a
motion and say, 'Hocus Pocus!'"

Immediately there was a loud clap of thunder and a
crashing bolt of lightning and all the children were
turned into frogs!
"I am a witch," groaned Bunya. "I *am* a witch!"
And Bunya the witch collapsed in a heap, sobbing, moaning,
wringing her hands, cracking her knuckles
and pounding the earth.

In the village square the great clock knelled the hour of six.
Bong, bong, bong, bong, bong, bong.
It was supper time. But instead of hungry children — frogs!

"A plague of locusts I've heard of," said an old man,
"a plague of frogs is a first."
Frogs! Frogs! Frogs! Everywhere frogs!

All the mothers and fathers were throwing frogs out of their houses as the frogs tried to sit down and eat their children's dinner. (Little realizing that the frogs *were* their children!) No sooner was a frog thrown out, than quick as a wink he jumped back in, only to be thrown out again.

Then the mayor of the village, who was a scholar and a very wise man, looked into the eyes of the frog who was trying to eat his son's supper. "This frog is our son!" he cried. "Our beloved Emile!"

So saying, he kissed his frog son and his eyes filled
with tears — as did the eyes of his frog son Emile.
"Let me kiss Emile too," said the mayor's wife.
"After all, I am this frog's mother!"
"Kiss, kiss," said the mayor, sobbing.
 Suddenly he tapped his head. "Aha!" he said. "I've got it!"

"Witchcraft!" he cried. "Courtesy of Bunya the witch."
So saying, the mayor clutched his frog son to his heart
and with his wailing wife behind him, ran into the streets
crying, "Bunya the witch has changed my darling son
Emile into a frog!"

"She's changed my sweet daughter Sophie," sobbed the butcher.
"A sweeter girl you couldn't find. Now she's a frog!"
"Bunya's changed my twin darlings into twin frogs!"
cried the baker.
And all the villagers ran out of their houses crying and
clutching their frog children.

They gathered in the village square. There was crying and wailing and gnashing of teeth and sad croaking from the frog children.

Then the mayor tapped his forehead again. "I've got an idea," he said, drying his tears and blowing his nose.
"Bunya the witch changed our children into frogs,
Bunya the witch can change our frogs back into children."

"Why didn't I think of that?" said the butcher.
"Because you're not as smart as I am," said the mayor.
"Don't argue," said the baker. "On to Bunya's!"
"On to Bunya's! On to Bunya's! On to Bunya's!"
chanted the villagers.

So with the mayor leading the way, all the mothers and fathers
marched to Bunya's tumble-down cottage on the edge of the village.
Bunya was still in a heap — sobbing, moaning, wringing her
hands, cracking her knuckles and pounding the earth.
"Bunya, you terrible witch," said the mayor, "you have done
a monstrous, horrible thing!"
"You're telling me," said Bunya. "I know, I know."

"But it's all a big mistake. I was trying to prove to your
children that I wasn't a witch. I made a motion.
I said 'Hocus Pocus'..."

Immediately there was a loud thunderclap and a crashing bolt of lightning and all the mothers and fathers turned into pigs!
"I've done it again!" groaned Bunya.

Poor Bunya was shaking so much, she went into the house to
make a glass of hot tea with lemon to calm her nerves.
"First frogs by mistake. Now pigs by mistake,"
groaned Bunya, as she sipped her hot tea with lemon.
"Croak, croak," croaked the frogs.
"Oink, oink," oinked the pigs.

"Such a racket," sighed Bunya. "Who needs all this trouble? Not me. After all these years, suddenly I'm a witch! Such a thing to discover at my age. Magic powers. Phfui! Who needs them?
But also who needs all these frogs and pigs?"
Then Bunya got an idea!

Bunya made a motion and said "Pocus Hocus!"

Immediately there was a loud thunderclap and a big bolt of lightning and all the frogs and pigs turned back into children and mothers and fathers!

The mothers and fathers were all very frightened
now that they knew from experience that Bunya
was a witch. They were also very respectful.
They inquired after her health and bowed and scraped,
trying not to displease Bunya in any way, so that Bunya
would not cast any more spells on them.
"Dear Bunya, I hope you are enjoying your old age,"
said the mayor.
"What's to enjoy?" replied Bunya.

"I'll send you a fresh chicken already plucked,
sweet Bunya," said the butcher.
"I'll send you some fresh day-old bread, kindly Bunya,"
said the baker.
"Has anyone ever told you you are a good looking old lady?"
said the wine merchant.
"Bunya, Bunya,
You're a peach!
Bunya, Bunya,
Make a speech!"
chanted all the children.

Bunya raised her hands to silence them.
"Please, Bunya, no more Hocus Pocus!" pleaded the mayor,
falling to his knees.
"Nobody's making Hocus Pocus!" said Bunya.
"I'm holding up my hands for silence. Now listen to me."

"I didn't need your insults.
I don't need your compliments.
Do me a favor, will you please?"
"Anything, anything you say, pretty Bunya," said the villagers.
"Stop calling me pretty Bunya and go home and mind your own business and let me mind mine, which happens to be being a witch."

"Whatever you say, good, sweet Bunya," replied the villagers, and they left walking backwards.

At last Bunya was alone. "So if I'm a witch, I'm a witch. Magic powers aren't the worst thing in the world to have. Maybe I could use them to help the poor, and who is poorer than poor Bunya? Nobody! There is one thing I have *always* wanted to do — travel. Now, in my old age, thanks to my magic powers, I can."

So Bunya the witch got on her broomstick and sailed away into the sky to see the world.

THE END